INCREDIBLE NED

by **BILL MAYNARD**

Illustrated by **FRANK REMKIEWICZ**

G. P. Putnam's Sons · New York

Incredible Ned. You could *see* what he said.
Every "thing" that he spoke appeared over his head,
Or right next to his chair. Or a few yards away,
And his friends would all shout:
"WE CAN *SEE* WHAT YOU SAY!"

When Ned said "gorilla," the kids all jumped back,
For they *saw* a gorilla and feared an attack.
And when Ned said "bananas," bananas were *there,*
On the stove, in the sink, in his hair, *everywhere!*

If a word that Ned said was the name of a "thing,"
Then that "thing" might float by on the end of a string!
He could say "and" or "the" and have nothing to fear,
It was words like "baboons" that made baboons appear.

It started when Ned was a child of one.

His father came home and asked, "What has Ned done?"

And his mother replied, "Well, it may sound absurd,

But today was the day that I saw his first word."

"You saw his first word?

You *saw* his first word?

YOU *SAW* HIS FIRST WORD?

Don't you really mean 'heard'?"

Ned's problems began on his first day of school:
Every time that he spoke he felt more like a fool
When the things that he said appeared over his head,
Or on top of his desk. Or a few rows away.

Then his classmates would shout:
"WE CAN *SEE* WHAT YOU SAY!"
When Ned said "giraffe," you could *see* a giraffe,
And its neck was so long it made everyone laugh.

When Ned said "parade," one appeared by the wall,

And marched straight through the class and out into the hall.

No wonder the children didn't get their books read:

It was so much more fun just to watch what Ned said.

Then his Teacher complained: "We're not getting *work* done.

With young Ned in the class, school is much too much fun.

I can't get him to stop. Every day it gets worse.

I will have to get help. Ned must go see the Nurse."

"Are you sick?" asked the Nurse. "Are you blowing your nose?
Have you started to sneeze? Are there pains in your toes?
Have you eaten too much? Have you had any spills?
You might need some time off, *or you could need some pills.*"

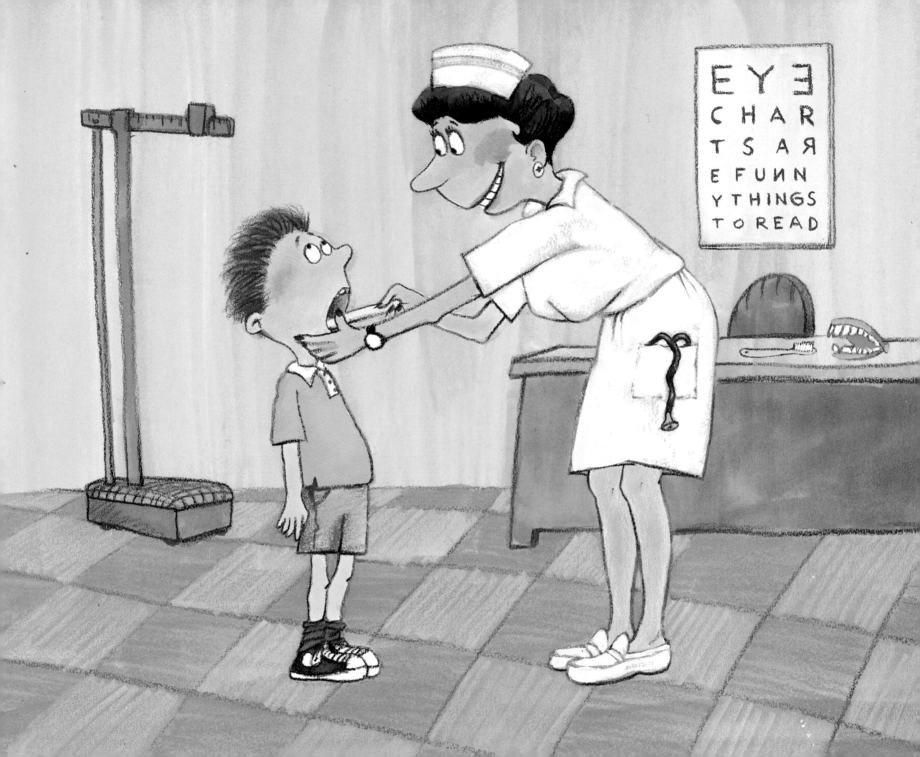

"Some pills?" said poor Ned, and the room quickly filled,
With some four million, three thousand, two hundred pills.
Pills that covered the desks and the chairs. What was worse,
There were so many pills that they covered the Nurse!

"I can't help," said the Nurse,
"though I'm glad Ned stopped by.
He's not sick. It's a trick.
Let the Band Leader try."

Maybe Ned's a musician, the Band Leader thought.
He might sing. He might play. He just needs to be taught.
When he asked Ned to name all the things in a band,
All the things filled the class. There was no place to stand.
"I can't cure him," he said. "And I think I know why.
It's his *words,* not his *notes.* Let the French Teacher try."

"*Zut!*" the French Teacher said. "Ned needs *new* things to say.
Words like *bon bon* for candy and *jouer* for play."
But when Ned said *"bateau"* (that's the French word for boat),

You could *see* a *bateau*. It was real! It could float!
And when Ned said *"voiture"* (that's the French word for car),
The class *saw* a *voiture*. This was going too far!

Ned's poor Teacher was now at the end of her rope.

So far no one had helped, but she had one last hope.

For there was one last someone who wasn't the same

So, she made one last call. And the *PRINCIPAL* came.

The Principal? Wow! That made Ned feel real sad.

When the Principal comes, then you know things are bad.

In your school, she's the law. In your school, she's the boss,

And the last thing you want is for her to feel cross.

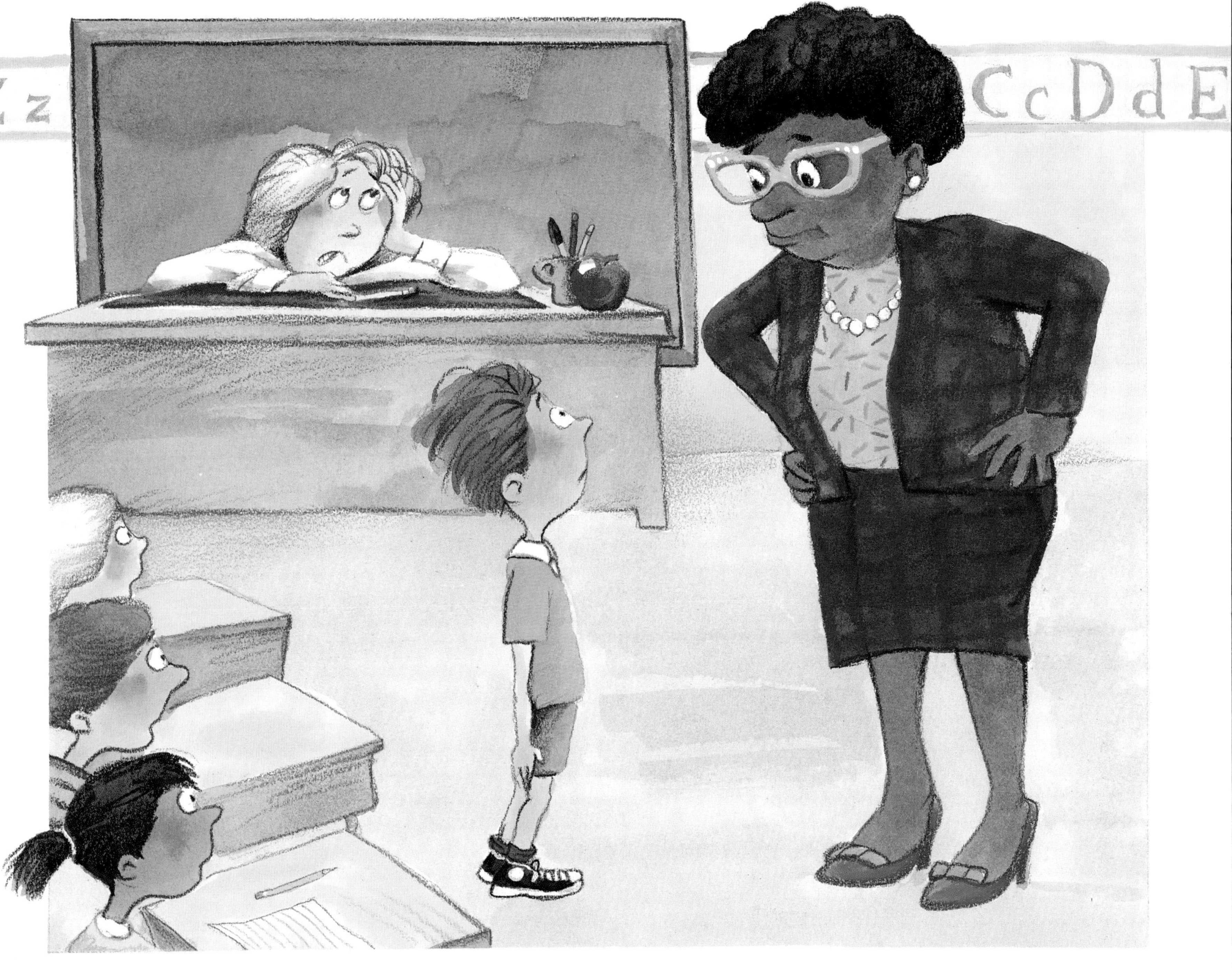
Zz
CcDdE

"Ned," the Principal said, "I will have to be stern,
For we want the class calm so the children can learn.
And whenever you speak, the whole class comes apart,
Since you can't seem to stop what you didn't mean to start.
I have made up a rule that should satisfy all:
YOU'LL SAY NOTHING AT ALL. OR GO STAND IN THE HALL."

Say nothing at all or go stand in the hall?

Ned must never say "bat"? Never even say "ball"?

"Then that's it!" Ned decided. "I guess I won't speak."

And he sat there in silence for almost a week.

'Til the Art Teacher came on her usual day,

And they told her why poor Ned had nothing to say.

"Oh, my goodness," she said. "Let me stop those complaints."

And she gave Ned some pencils and paper and paints.

Then she watched what Ned did, and she liked what she saw
When he picked up a pencil and started to draw.
He drew fish. He drew birds. He drew flowers and trees.
He drew lions and tigers and monkeys and bees.

"What is that?" asked the Teacher. "A lion," said Ned.
  And *nothing*, but *nothing,* showed over his head.
"What is that?" asked the Teacher. "A tree," Ned replied.
  And *nothing,* but *nothing,* appeared at his side.
  The Art Teacher smiled. She could understand Ned.
  And she knew why those things had shown over his head.
"Ned's an artist," she said. "That's what Ned's all about.
  When your head's full of pictures, they have to come out."

times, when young Ned is at home late at night,
n he's opened his window and turned out his light,
his pens put away and his paints on the shelf,
n he's sure he's alone, he'll say "moose" to himself.
a moose will appear at the foot of his bed
d he'll know that he still is *Incredible Ned*.

Now to show those great pictures that lived in his head,

Ned didn't need to use words. He could draw them instead.

(Because painting and talking are equally real.

They're just two different ways to show folks how you feel.)

And as long as Ned colored and painted and drew,

He could speak just like me. He could talk just like you.

And *nothing* he said appeared over his head,

Or right next to his desk or a few yards away.

And his classmates complained: "We can't see what you say."

For Billy and Hannah, Sarah,
Elvis and Wyatt, and Luke. – B. M.

For all the art teachers,
may their numbers increase. – F. R.

G. P. Putnam's Sons, a division of The Putnam & Grosset Group, 200 Madison Avenue, New York, NY 10016. G. P. Putnam's Sons, Reg. U.S. Pat. & Tm. Off. Published simultaneously in Canada. Printed in Singapore. Book design by Cecilia Yung and Donna Mark. Text set in Icone. Library of Congress Cataloging-in-Publication Data. Maynard, Bill. Incredible Ned/Bill Maynard; illustrated by Frank Remkiewicz. p. cm. Summary: The things Ned speaks of become reality, until a knowing art teacher solves his problem with paper and paints. [1. Artists—Fiction. 2. Stories in rhyme.] I. Remkiewicz, Frank, ill. II. Title. PZ8.3.M455In 1997 [Fic]—dc20 95-53753 CIP AC ISBN 0-399-23023-8 10 9 8 7 6 5 4 3 2 1 FIRST IMPRESSION